With All my Love

With All my Love

Donald Readerlear

To order additional copies of this book, contact:
Xlibris
NZ TFN: 0800 008 756 (Toll Free inside the NZ)
NZ Local: 9-801 1905 (+64 9801 1905 from outside New Zealand)
www.Xlibris.co.nz
Orders@Xlibris.co.nz
839425

CHAPTER 1

Grace looked into her mother's eyes. All she could see was sheer love.

Eve stared at the wonder in her arms.

"Mummy loves you so very much. Now Mummy has got to murder Daddy."

***

Eve was born 14 February in Te Awamutu on a farm. Her parents Ellen and Mark were share milkers. Eve and Allen were married at the age of 19. It wasn't unusual for a girl in the country to marry early. Eve and Allen set up home in Grey Lynn, Auckland. Allen had been given a transfer from Te Awamutu Farmers Store to the city of Auckland. They were a happy couple.

After they had moved to Grey Lynn, Allen started his new job; circumstances were fine. Eve was careful with what she spent; they were a normal married couple trying so very hard to save enough money to put a deposit on a house. Eventually, they managed to buy a house in Grey Lynn. But they had a big mortgage on it.

The rot set in. When Allen came home late from work, he had spent a few hours with the boys drinking. Eve had cooked his favourite meal, steak and kidney pie, but because Allen was late home, it was burnt, and she was cross with him for not letting her know he would be late. She didn't mind that he was out with the boys, just that he didn't let her know.

"Allen, why didn't you let me know you would be late? Then the meal that I have taken so long to cook wouldn't be spoilt."

"You don't tell me if and when I want to go out with the boys."

"That's not the point. You could have let me know. But all you could think of was going out drinking. I think that is very selfish."

The whole argument got far worse. It ended up with Allen slapping Eve on the face, and he also picked up the meal and threw it at her, hitting her on the side of her head. Blood poured out of the wound; she was crying, and she ran up the stairs to their bedroom. She flung herself on the bed. Allen came to the top of the stairs in a terrible rage, couldn't open the door to the bedroom, so he kicked it in. She screamed at him to get out. He stood their looking down at her. He took his belt off and flung it to the wall; it made a clatter as it hit the wall. She screamed at him again to get out of the bedroom. He stood perfectly still watching her scream at him; he grabbed her arm, twisted it. She screamed in pain; he pushed her firmly down on the bed. Then he raped his wife.

The morning was bright, a perfect morning; the birds sang, the sun glinted through the open windows. Allen had already gone to work, and Eve got up to tend to Grace, their daughter.

"Oh! My darling daughter, today I am so sorry to say your mummy will start to poison your daddy? Then once it's finished, you and I will have a happy life. Oh. My sweet baby, it's the only way out, Grace."

Grace looked at her adoring mother, not understanding what Eve had to put up with when she was pregnant. Allen had become even more violent with Eve. And once Grace was born, he hated her because every time he looked at her, he knew the child had been created by his rape of her mother.

So Eve knew this would be the only way out, so slowly, she fed him arsenic a little at a time; bit by bit, she poisoned Allen. He got ill and weak. He visited the doctor. The doctor thought it might be colitis. He had arranged for Allen to see a specialist. Eve knew then she would need to up the doses of the arsenic so that Allen would be either too ill or dead. As time went by, he took to his bed. Eve nursed him with great care, even sometimes feeling sorry for him, but her will was strong; she knew there was no way out.

Then he passed away. The funeral was sad. She, the widow, was upset, not for murdering her husband but for her and her baby. Who would look after them now? Eve needed to find another husband.

But this time Eve was determined that he would be able to take care of herself and Grace.

Eve started to work at a tie and shirt factory in Grey Lynn. She was a keen worker, did as much overtime as she could. The owner, Steven Hutton, was a widower of ten years; his wife had died in child birth, and the little girl she had given birth to very quickly fell ill and died. He now was 49. He had noticed that this new woman working for him was a good worker.

Every Christmas he would buy hams for each of his staff. This Christmas Eve was sick at home, so Steven brought the ham to her address. Eve had thanked him for delivering the ham and invited him to their Christmas dinner.

"You live here with your daughter. No husband?"

She looked sad when Steven said this. She looked down at her plate as if trying to answer him as best she could. "Mr Hutton—"

"I think you should call me Steven. Or Steve."

She cleared her throat. "Um, Steven. Oh, I am so sorry. I am not used to calling you by your christen name."

He could see she was having trouble with trying to be informal with him. She was such a good-looking woman of about, he thought, late 20s with a child; how on earth can she manage her affairs? He placed his hand on hers as he spoke. "I am sorry I have put you into this position. But, Eve—" Then he thought again. "May I call you Eve?"

She pulled her hand away from his, and she looked so pure and so very much alone. "Yes, you may."

That was their first meeting; their friendship developed over the coming weeks and months. Whenever he came down from his office in the factory, he would find her. Steven found that she was a kind and hardworking woman, and gradually, their friendship changed to a much closer arrangement. Whenever it was Grace's birthday, he would buy the little girl an expensive present. Grace was now three years old and, oh, so much the child he had lost.

One evening, whilst Steven was in his large house in Balmoral, thinking about Eve and Grace, he suddenly came up with the plan of marriage: How would he approach Eve? How would he pose the proposal to her? How was he going to get her to agree to marrying him? He was twenty years her senior. He knew he had to try because he had fallen in love with Eve and her daughter Grace.

Of course, all this time, Eve was really manipulating Steven, making him think she was vulnerable, and knew, sooner or later, he would ask her to marry him. She would, at first, refuse his proposal, stating that she couldn't accept because she was far too proud. But she also knew this would only make him more determined to marry her. Eventually, she said she would marry him. The idea of being Mrs Eve Hutton, the wife of the owner of a tie and shirt manufacturing business, having a large house in a very posh part of Auckland, she would be his wife and rich . . .

There was one fly in the ointment: Steven had an elder sister, Brenda. Brenda didn't like Eve one tiny bit. Her opinion of Eve was that she was an upstart and only wanted to get hold of her brother's wealth, which was the case with Eve. Both women disliked each other. Brenda knew she could do nothing to stop her brother from marrying Eve; she had tried and failed. One day Brenda had a dreadful argument with her brother.

"Steve, can't you see she is only after your money?"

"And what if Eve is, Brenda?"

"So it's Eve this, Eve that, you're besotted with her? Your twenty years older than her. You are old enough to be her father."

"What if I am, Brenda? You're only jealous because you missed your chance of marriage to that bloody idiot Frank! Thank God, Dad made you open your eyes."

As Steven said this, he realised he had hurt Brenda; she had given up a happy life with Frank all because Jack, their father, had taken a dislike to Frank and didn't wish to see him as his daughter's husband. Brenda broke down. "How could you say that, Steven? You are so unkind. I loved him."

Steven bent down over his weeping sister. "I am so sorry, Brenda. I know you could be right about Eve. But I love her and her daughter. It's my chance of being happy again. When I am with her, I don't think I am so old. She makes me happy."

"I know. Steven, maybe I am jealous of her. I love you so much. I can't bear that you might be hurt again."

"Brenda, I love her. But I love you too. If you say no, then I will not marry her."

Brenda looked up to her brother, how much she loved him; even as children, she took care of him. The very idea that some strange woman would take over from her . . .

But she also knew he loved her, so he needed her support. "Steven, marry her, please."

But deep in her heart, she felt something wasn't quite right with Eve; her feminine intuition told her not to trust Eve at all.

Steven and Eve got engaged in the spring. By winter, they were married. Eve became the mistress of a large home in Balmoral. Riches suited her; she soon asked her husband Steven for a car, not just any car but an expensive one. Eve said she was embarrassed taking Grace to school on the bus. Eve got on with the staff. Eve had noticed one or more of the staff working harder than the rest. She convinced Steven that it was a good policy to reward such hard work with increases to their wages; this made her very popular. Plus, Steven could see that Eve was slowly understanding how to get the staff to work harder. Eve revelled in her popularity. The outcome was that she could get the staff to do anything; they loved her. This was her plan.

Eve's relationship with Steven's sister Brenda still wasn't very good. Eve thought of a plan to win her over. She spent more time with her sometime, weeding her garden, helping do the chores in the house, generally making herself wanted. Eve had a plan of her own. Eve could see, no matter how much she tried to win over Brenda, she knew Brenda still did not trust her.

One sunny summer day Eve was sitting in her garden with a gin and tonic, mulling over what she could do next to ingratiate herself with Brenda. Eve had, more or less, decided that maybe a new course might need to be taken. Brenda would always be a problem, so she must go.

CHAPTER 2

For the next few weeks Eve couldn't think straight. Steven noticed his wife seemed unhappy or maybe not her bright happy self; she seemed preoccupied.

Steven was at their kitchen table eating breakfast. How was he going to approach his wife? He knew something was not right, but what?

"Eve, are you okay?"

"Yes!"

"Tell me, what's up? I know something's not right. I can't bear it when you're sad."

"I'm fine."

"You're not, love. Tell me, Eve."

She started crying. He cradled her in his arms She spluttered an answer. "Steven . . ." More tears shed. "Oh! Steven, I have missed my monthly periods, I'm not sure, but . . ." Once again, more tears.

"Eve, what a clever wife you are. Do you think you are . . ."

Then Eve really cried; she sobbed. "I'm pregnant, Steven!"

Steven couldn't have been happier to have a child of his own at the age of 50; this was triumphant. He was going to be a father. "My pretty young wife."

In no time, Steven had blurted out at an office meeting that Eve was pregnant. And he wasted no time in telling his sister. She was relatively happy for him. But still, there was something inside telling her not to trust Eve.

Now what, and how was she going to get rid of Brenda? She didn't want to use arsenic this time; she thought she could be a little more inventive. Eve took her time. All this time, the staff were generally happy for the married couple Steven was the happiest he had ever known. Eve was at home one day, looking through the windows of her home; she pulled back the curtains to look at the garden. Steven had a way with plants and colours; he had a lovely bed of foxgloves, all different shades. Then it came to her. She blurted out, "Digitalis! That might do the trick!"

The house had a large library collected by Steven's father and grandfather. Eve spent that day going through all sorts of books 'til she came to a very dusty volume, a book that was tucked in at the end of a shelf. Eve sat into an armchair with the book on her lap, reading all about poisons and their effects. Eve read foxgloves digitalis, if ingested, has the following symptoms: nausea, diarrhoea, vomiting, headache, dizziness, skin rash.

As the list was getting longer, the more Eve was getting excited; rapid heartbeat, mental changes.

Eve asked herself, "How would I make it? What would it taste like?" Then out loud. "Soup! That's it."

Eve felt very pleased with herself. She could, as it were, kill two birds with one stone: poison Brenda and with her death, have Steven to herself.

First of all, she needed a strong soup flavour. Eve went through all her recipe books, flipping over page after page, then she came across the perfect soup.

Chicken or beetroot or a maybe a mixed vegetable. In the next few weeks, Eve quizzed her husband as to what did he think was Brenda's favourite soup. It turned out Brenda couldn't stand beetroot at all. So here Eve was, she could use chicken and vegetable soup. Over the next few weeks, she practised. The one thing about murder was the planning; the lead-up to the actual and the final act was so exciting. Eve bustled around her kitchen, sometimes humming her favourite tune.

The preparation of the digitalis was the next problem: how to do it. Once again, Eve got all the detail from the book she had found in the library. After Eve had prepared the digitalis, next problem was how much to use in the soup. Would it change the flavour of the soup? So it really was a matter of trial and error. Anyway, Eve cleaned the kitchen up, put the parts of the foxglove plant that she hadn't used in to the kitchen bin under the sink, turned the element off, and left the saucepan on top of the stove on an element near the front of the stove. Eve felt quite pleased with herself as she sat in her favourite armchair in the lounge and fell asleep.

Steven came home early; he had been to the local florist and had brought a bouquet of red roses for Eve. Quite often, he brought small presents home for Eve. Eve had fallen into a very happy situation with Steven; he was attentive, kind, and Eve truly liked him, but that sister of his, she had to go. Steven stole into their kitchen using the back door; he wanted to surprise his happy wife. Then he smelt the chicken soup on the stove, and knowing his wife was such a good cook and regularly came up with all sorts of cakes, fruit loaves, all sorts of taste morsel for him, he naturally thought the soup was for him. *Shall I wait until Eve dishes this soup up for the family, or should I try some?*

Almost as if he were a naughty boy, he took a soup spoon out of the cutlery draw. He took one spoonful then another, revelling in the subtle flavours of the soup, little realising Eve had laced the soup with digitalis. Eventually, he felt quite full and a bit angry with himself for being so greedy, but he knew Eve was such a loving woman; he knew he could get away with nearly anything. As he walked to the lounge and saw her asleep in the armchair, with her hand on her stomach, almost in a protective way over their baby, he thought how lovely she was and married to him, an old man. He suddenly blurted out, "I love you, my queen of hearts."

Eve awoke to Steven leaning over her; she saw the red roses. "For me?"

"Yes, my queen!" He made a mock bow and got on one knee. "If I were not your husband, I would ask you to marry me at this very moment. When is my Grace coming home from school?"

"And why would my prince wish to know?"

He took her hand in his. "Ha! Ha! Sweet maid, your prince wants to make love to his sweet wife." Then he suddenly doubled up with pain.

Eve looked at him in shock. "What's up, Steven?"

Steven, gripping his stomach, slipped onto the floor. "I don't feel well, darling. My chest, it feels strange? My stomach is so sore . . ."

All Eve could do was look at him in horror with her hand over her mouth, letting out a gurgled scream. "Steven! Steven! Oh! My god!"

He was still on his knees but was on the point of toppling over; Eve flung herself onto the floor next to him, grabbing him in her arms. Steven's heart started missing beats. He knew he had always had a dicky heart; his doctor had informed him of this just before he married Eve but never did he ever think it was that bad. "It's my heart, Eve. I'm having a heart attack, I think. It feels odd. Get the doctor!"

Eve wasn't sure quite what to do, but one thing she knew: Steven must have eaten some of the poison-laced soup. She rushed into the kitchen. Then she saw Steven had eaten a lot of soup.

Now what was she to do? She grabbed the rubbish bin from under the kitchen sink, tied it up, ran outside to her car, opened the boot, threw the bag in, then rushed back to Steven. Eve found him on his back, his eyes staring into space She felt his pulse—nothing. She sat back on her bottom and swayed back and forth, screaming.

Fiona came in; she had just picked up Grace from school. The little girl ran into the house then suddenly skidded to a halt as she saw her daddy lying on his back on the floor with her mummy rocking back and forth, screaming. Fiona saw the mayhem. She acted quickly, ran to the phone and rang the doctor, and came back to Eve. She could see that Steven looked as if he had passed away. Eve clutched Steven's hand; the sweet perfume of the roses wafted into her nose. They were scattered around Eve and Steven.

Eve awoke in her bed. The doctor sat next to her; he held her hand. "I'm so sorry, Eve, but Steven has passed away."

"Oh! No! No!"

"Also, Eve, I'm afraid you have lost your baby."

Eve rose out of her bed, screaming, clutching her stomach. "No! No! This is all my fault!"

"I am sorry, my dear. It happens sometimes with extreme grief."

The next few days were a blur. She didn't eat or sleep, even though the doctor gave her sedatives.

But there was one thing she needed to do: get rid of the rubbish bag in the boot.

Even though the doctor had told her that her husband Steven had died of a massive heart attack, she knew she had murdered her own husband.

Two days later, Eve waited 'til midnight, making sure all her neighbours' lights were out; she crept out, got into her car, let the brake off, and glided down to the road. Then she started the ignition, stayed there for a short time, then drove off. Eve drove to the factory; outside was a very large bin due to be picked up by the city council the following morning. Eve got out of the car, opened the top off the bin, got the rubbish bag out of the car boot, threw it into the bin, closed the lid, got back into her car, drove a short way, then stopped the car.

"Steven, if you can hear me, I am so sorry!" Eve cried.

Then she drove home, parked into her garage, and went up the stairs to see if Grace was asleep. Then Eve crept downstairs and sat in her armchair and fell asleep.

The days went by. Brenda was so kind to Eve, and all her misgivings about Eve had been blown away when she knew that the poor-stricken woman had not only lost her husband but she also lost their child. Brenda was mortified. She had not only lost her beloved brother but also the child Eve was carrying.

The next year saw Eve having a nervous breakdown. This was where Brenda became the stalwart of the family; all her misgivings about Eve were forgotten. Between herself and Fiona, Eve's friend, they helped Eve back to health.

CHAPTER 3

Ann and Henry Chivers were Baptists. They had one son, Martin; he grew up tall with wavy jet-black hair and the bluest eyes you could ever imagine, deep pools of fathomless blue. He grew up to be a happy youth and blossomed into manhood. Ann and Henry sorted a worthy bride for him in their church.

There were a number of very pretty girls but none that had wealthy families, for they wanted their son to marry into wealth. There was one girl whose parents owned a bread shop in the high street of Mata Mata, but she was plain and with a rather unpleasant personality. Iris was known to have a very bad temper if she didn't get her way She was an only child of Julia and Brendon Salt. She was a spoilt brat, they gave her whatever she wanted, and if she didn't get exactly what she wanted, she used to scream and yell, so eventually, Julia and her husband Brendon gave in.

Ann and her husband knew this wasn't quite the best choice. But as Ann told her husband, that Martin being such a kind, loving son, he would be able to tame Iris; both parents arranged for the two young ones to meet. As soon as Iris met Martin, she wanted him, mostly because she had noted that the other girls in their church were all over Martin. So she was determined to marry him whatever the obstacles were.

They were married; they seemed happy. Soon Iris became pregnant. Then the problems started. She was nasty, cruel, and vicious to her husband. Everything that Martin did was wrong. She eventually gave birth to a boy. Then one night, when she was having her usually tirade of anger, Iris blurted out that the child was not his. Martin felt a cold he had never felt before set into him. Eventually, he realised it was hate. Yes, a hate that whenever he saw Iris, it curdled and spiralled deep inside him. He loved his son; the baby was all he had ever wanted. He would sit admiring James in his cot, the child's fingers curdled around his, and Martin's heart jumped for joy. This was all he wanted. His hatred for Iris was complete, but Martin had made his mind up that he would have to put up with Iris's nasty personality for James's sake.

The family had taken a few days off to visit some of Martin's cousins in Thames. One morning, just after Thames had been hit with an extreme storm, Martin, Iris, James, and Martin's cousin Dotty went for a short walk along the flood banks of the quick-flowing river that emptied into the Firth of Thames.

Iris was in one of her better moods, mostly because of Dotty. Dotty was quite a kind soul, and somehow she was able to control some of Iris's bad tempers. At first, everything seemed happy; the sun shone, the water fowls dipped in and out of the fast-flowing river. Martin had taken James out of the carry cot Iris was wheeling him in.

"Iris, look at those ducks swimming in that fast-flowing water?"

Iris shouted at Martin. Dotty put her hand on Iris's arm to try to calm her down but not this time. "What on earth do you mean? Those are not bloody ducks. They're shags! Any idiot can see they are not ducks."

She went on and on at Martin, until eventually he lost his temper with her and shouted at her, "Shut! Up!"

And that was it; she turned on him, even though he was trying to shield the screaming baby. Iris hit him around the face; he stumbled, almost dropped the child, then everything raced ahead. Iris, in her anger, had reach over and slapped Martin around the face, but she hadn't realise she had put one foot between the wheels of the carry cot. Iris stumbled, bumped into her husband, who, by now, was skidding down the embankment into the river. She followed but dragged the carry cot with her, both entered the swift flowing river with one enormous splash. Dotty screamed and had made a grab for the crying child before both parents fell into the river. Luckily, they were near to the one-lane bridge across the river into the main town of Thames. Dotty shouted up to a man standing at the bridge's handrail. He suddenly saw the commotion. He ran across the bridge to a small wooden housing that had a red and white safety buoy in it. He grabbed it and hurled it into the river as near to one of the people as he could. Martin made a grab for it and tried to swim to his wife Iris, who was being pulled under by the carry cot wheels she was entangled in. Martin could see Iris was being pulled under by the weight of it. Iris disappeared once then bobbed back up again. She screamed at Martin, "Come on, you idiot, save me, you stupid man!"

Then something in his head said, "Save yourself," so he did and let Iris be dragged down to the depths to be drowned. He was free at last of this monster. He struck off firmly to the banks, dragged himself up the flood embankment. Wet and shivering, He looked up to the sky, put his hands together in silent prayer for his drowned wife and for himself. He shouted out to the heavens, "Free! I'm free!"

Then he looked around to see if anyone had heard him. He was alone on the other side of the river far away from the bridge; no one had heard.

After the funeral, Martin found his life had completely changed; no arguments, no stepping on eggshells. His son James was his only reason to live; he put all his effort and love in bringing up his son.

He decided to move away from the town he was born in; there were too many bad memories. At first, he rented a small flat on the slopes of Cornwell Park from an elderly widow, Marie Grove; her husband had died many years ago. Marie was childless, and this handsome young man and his sweet son of about three years old were a dream come true. Marie lavished love on them. Unbeknownst to Martin, she had altered her will, leaving him everything she owned.

Martin had got a job working for the post office in the city of Auckland. Most days he would use the train to get to work. Once he had enough money, he bought a small car. His life was happy. He neither thought or cared about the past and didn't consider that he should have tried to save his wife; besides, he hated her. Even the memory of her, he had washed from his memory.

Marie passed away one summer evening, sitting in her chair watching the clouds scurrying across the sky. It happened so quickly; here one moment, gone the next. True to her word, Martin was left everything. Now he had a house, car, and money in the bank, not a great deal of money but enough for him and James.

He met and married Jenny, not a beauty but a kindly soul, or so he thought.

Once married, she started bullying him. "You need to do more overtime. I need more money in the bank. We have bills to pay. James has just started intermediate school. He needs books and clothes."

The list went on and on. Jenny had stopped working; Martin was working every hour he could. She wanted a new house. She had seen a section just the other side of Mount Roskill in a new subdivision. She bullied Martin in to buying it. Then the house had to be just right. One night she nagged and nagged Martin with one requirement for the house then another. James had been having a stay over with his friends the twins, Gavin and Mark. Martin and his wife were in the kitchen. Jenny was as usual, grumbling about this and that, arguing with Martin, accusing him of being a lazybones, when something inside Martin snapped; he picked the frying pan that Jenny had left on the stove element. And with all his force, he brought it down on top of Jenny's head; at first, she stopped nagging, then her eyes looked at Martin in surprise, then she slumped to the floor. Martin stood over her with the frying pan in his right hand. He thought, *What have I done?*

In total quiet, he very carefully put the frying pan back onto the stove element, bent down to see if she were dead or just unconscious. He felt her pulse; there was nothing. He sat into one of the kitchen chairs for a moment, thinking of nothing. Then an idea came to him: At the new house, the builders were going to lay the main floor with concrete, so he rolled Jenny in one of their old carpets, went out to his garage which was on the side of the house, turned all the lights off, then slung the carpet and Jenny over his shoulder. This was easy because Jenny was a short thin woman and he was 6 feet tall and very muscular. He put her into the boot, backed out of his driveway, and drove to the subdivision and the house. He had already told the builder, a friend of his, that he would help him with the laying of the concrete that following morning. Martin thought if he said he had started already, the following day Greg would think nothing of it. He pulled the dead body of Jenny out and in to the area where they were to set the concrete. Martin pulled the dead body out of the carpet, only to find Jenny was coming to. He grabbed a long-handled spade and hit her 'til she was dead then started to lay the concrete over his wife. He didn't finish the whole area. He cleaned the blood off the spade, threw the old rag into his car, and drove back home.

The next morning he woke up as if nothing had happened; he made his breakfast, cleaned the house, made the bed, and drove over to help Greg and his workmen finish off the concrete-laying. Greg had said to him that he didn't need to start the concreting the previous night, but Martin said he was on his own as Jenny had left to see her aunty in Wellington the previous morning and would be away for some time, so he said he didn't want to stay in his empty home, so rather than that, he did some concreting that evening.

Martin got home that day very tried, but he knew James would be coming home that afternoon, and he needed to get his story correct for his son.

James came home with the twins in tow. "Dad, where's Mum?"

Greg and Mark were already making their way upstairs to James's bedroom. He had told them the previous night that his dad had just brought him a new engine for his train set and wanted to show the twins.

"Mum's not here son." Martin hesitated as he told James a miss truth. He hated telling a miss truth, but this was important; he must start out with a plausible lie and not too complicated because he would need to keep the story the same for everyone.

"Mum's gone to see Aunty Shelly."

"When is Mum coming back, Dad?"

"All these questions. She's only just gone."

Anyway, James soon forgot and raced upstairs to play with the train set.

The days went to weeks then months. Martin thought, *Maybe I give Shelly a ring, ask to talk to Jenny, of course, knowing full well she was dead.*

Shelly's husband Burt answered the phone. Martin talked with Bert for some time, chatting about the All Blacks win against the Aussies that weekend. Then he asked to speak to his wife.

"She's not here, Martin. Was she supposed to come down here?"

"Yes." Martin said this and tried to make it sound as surprised as he could.

"Na. She is not here. Do you want to speak to Shelly?"

"Yes."

"Shell, Martin's on the phone, wants to know where Jenny is."

Martin could hear Shelly and her husband talking about Jenny.

"Do you know where she is, Shell?"

"Hun, I have not heard from her for weeks?"

Then Shelly came on the phone. "Hello, love. Why did you think Jenny was here?"

Now Martin had to be very careful in getting his story spot on because from now on, the police would be involved. He approached the whole story with care. He told Shell that they had an argument, Jenny had stormed out, saying she was staying with Shelly and her husband until Martin had cooled down. Shelly once again said she and Bert knew nothing, not a single thing. She suggested Martin contact the train booking office to see if Jenny had bought a ticket down to Wellington. Before Martin put the receiver down, he promised he would keep them informed of what transpired.

Martin know rang the train booking office, of course, knowing Jenny was under heavy concrete in his new house. Then he rang the police, telling them the whole story. The sergeant on duty at the time asked Martin had his wife gone somewhere else. He replied no. Anyway, the police said they would start to look for her. After several months of investigation, the detective handling the case came around to see Martin at his home. The detective sat in the lounge of Martin.

"I'm very sorry, Mr Chivers, we have found nothing, so I'm afraid we now have to say Mrs Jenny Susan Chivers is now a missing person's case . . ." The detective paused for some time so that Mr Chivers could take it all in. He knew these sorts of cases normally ended by the said husband finding out later that his little wifey had gone off with another man. But he didn't think it was wise to alert this young man. He felt he was such a nice young man. The detective, Brian Stiles, was usually able to trust his intuition, and this was no exception.

Months went into years, Martin got older, and James grew into a tall somewhat gangly youth with a ready smile, dark hair, and happy.

Martin and his son had moved into their new house, and James was busy planning out the gardens and pathways. The lad was a natural gardener, knew which plant would go well. There was only one tree that James was not happy with; it was a wattle. He had planted it far too close to the lounge, and the tree had found some sort of extra nourishment from somewhere. Of course, James didn't realise that the nourishment was from Jenny's decomposing body.

CHAPTER 4

Grace was now 20, quite tall, slim, with long blond hair and green eyes—a stunner. Her mother Eve doted on her, and her Aunty Brenda was so proud of the young girl; apart from being a pretty young girl, she was intelligent, studying at university. She was thinking about becoming a nurse. Eve and Brenda had become inseparable. The old lady was getting frail and relied on Eve for everything, never suspecting Eve had killed her beloved brother Steven. Life carried on. Eve managed the factory exceptionally well, increasing production, making alliances with other clothing manufacturers, opening up other factories, branching out into ladies' fashion items, in fact becoming an astute businesswoman; whereas Brenda knew she was coming to the end of her life. Brenda had one last wish, that she be laid next to her brother when she passes away. In the summer of that year, Brenda passed away peacefully with even Eve generally upset.

The years went by. Grace was seeing Cuthbert, a slim and very self-centred young man; he came from a very wealthy and old Auckland family. They married and had one son, Giles, a sunny child. Everything was relatively sunny; Cuthbert wasn't the easiest man to live with. He was selfish and extremely lazy. He always made sure his wife and son had plenty of money because his family were rich and well connected in Auckland society.

Eve was very pleased about that, going to many important functions, being part of the right members of Auckland's high society.

His one and only love was the sea; he had a yacht and sailed her in the gulf. Sometimes away for days at a time, Grace had complained about him many times to Eve, about his lazy attitude and cold nature with her. Eve, in return, consoled her daughter.

"Mum, all he thinks about is that yacht of his!"

"Grace, don't you think you are overreacting?"

"Maybe, Mum. Our relationship isn't the same as it used to be."

Eve was listening to Grace, but—and it was a big but—Eve was very aware of how much Cuthbert was doted on by his parents, Pamela and Oswald Downer. Grace being married to Cuthbert and his well-to-do parents, it frankly helped with the factory; she got more orders, not only shops but also department stores in the city. Business hadn't been better. Eve wasn't going to rock the boat, so Eve took a more conciliatory attitude; Eve let things slide.

One day her daughter came grumbling to her about Cuthbert. "Mum, I think sometimes you are not listening to me."

"Grace, please don't say that."

"Sometimes I think you think more of the business than me."

Eve didn't answer her daughter; she knew Grace was correct. Eve was concerned more about the business and the connections with Cuthbert's family. Eve also knew her duty was with her daughter. Eve knew, sooner or later, she would have to do something about Cuthbert.

Her answer wasn't quite what her daughter hoped for; in fact, once again, it almost looked as if her mother was trying to fob her off again. It wasn't the fact Eve knew just what to do with her son-in-law, something that was near to his heart. Eve would need to tread carefully and plan his demise.

"My dear, your mother will sort things out for you. I'll talk with Pamela and Oswald." Which Eve did, but Pamela thought Cuthbert needed his freedom and felt he needed the sea air, and in time, he would come up to Eve's standards.

Eve actually knew she wouldn't get anywhere with Cuthbert's parents, but she knew it would be a good idea to seem to get them on board. Besides, there were far more important things to sort out before she could put her plans into action.

Eve had spent many hours in the local library, reading up about sailing and the particular yacht Cuthbert sailed.

At last, Eve felt she was ready. Eve had been chatting far more with her son-in-law, asking him this and that about sailing. And how much she let him believe she was interested in going on a trip with him, knowing full well Grace would never dream of going sailing because she gets seasick and had tried vainly to join her husband on the boat.

Eve picked a September day. Eve had asked Cuthbert if she could sail with him the next day, asking—no, begging—Cuthbert to sail to the Great Barrier island, quite a large island in the Hauraki Gulf. Cuthbert was, for a change, excited about the fact that someone actually found his nautical stuff interesting. His opinion of Eve was such that he felt Eve was a genuine friend, not his mother-in-law.

He was more than keen to have her on board. All four went to the place where Cuthbert moored the yacht. Grace drove with her son Giles next to her, chattering all the time with his grandmother, Eve sitting next to Cuthbert in the back of the car.

"Mum?" Giles had been badgering his mother and father since the night before, then in the morning, and now having another go at his mother.

Answering her son quickly, "Once again, Giles, the answer is no!"

"Ah, Mum—"

"Giles, I'm not going to change my mind. No. And that's my final word. I really mean it."

Eve could see, sooner or later, her daughter Grace would give in, and she couldn't have that; what she had planned for Cuthbert, Eve needed to be alone with Cuthbert on his yacht.

Eve took Giles to one side. "Giles, I need you to do something for me."

This got the young boy's attention; he turned his head around to face his grandmother. "Yes."

"Giles, just this once, I need you to look after Mummy."

"Oh, Nana."

"Giles, this is important. I need you to look after Mummy just this once." Eve looked at her grandson. She had a way with getting her own way, so a small child was nothing. Eve pointed to herself as she explained to the child. "Please, for me."

"Oh, Nana, do I have to?"

"Giles, I wouldn't ask you if I wasn't sure you would do a good job of it."

Eve had won. The young boy was putty in her hand. Eve knew he dearly wanted to go on the yacht with his dad but not this time. What Eve had planned for his father was for his father alone.

They eventually came to the yacht mooring. The day was bright with a touch of a wind not much.

They got on board, shifted all the items that they would need for the day sailing. Cuthbert had arranged for an overnight stay in a small bach that his family owned in Port Fitzroy, one of the main settlements on the Great Barrier Island. They said goodbye, waved as the yacht flew out into the ocean.

Cuthbert could see by Eve's familiarity with his yacht that she was very sure at what she was doing. He shouted different orders to put the main sail up. Eve did it quickly. Eve felt the wind in her hair; she felt so alive, then realising what this meant to Cuthbert. He had, as soon as they were on board the yacht, came alive; and Eve had to admit she felt his friendship for her was genuine and vice versa. Eve got wet from the spray, so did Cuthbert; they were happy in each other's company, laughing. The time went so quick. Eventually, they turned into the harbour leading to Port Fitzroy. This was where Cuthbert said this part of the lead in to docking was hard because of the many shoals, deep areas, and shallow parts, where only his experience would be needed. All the time, Eve was making close attention to details. They anchored the yacht, brought everything to the deck. Eve made sure that the thermos flask was with her because the following morning she would need to warm it up for Cuthbert for the return sailing.

Cuthbert rowed the small rowing boat to shore. They lugged everything up a small hill to the family's bach.

"Listen to the birds. Is that a bell bird?"

"Yep!"

"Cuthbert, it's heaven. Grace doesn't realise what she is missing. Please, Cuthbert, we must make sure the next trip I'll make sure she comes."

Cuthbert response was slightly offhand. "I've tried." And he shrugged.

"I'm sure you know we can win her over."

He seemed happy with Eve's suggestion. Anyway, it was quite late. Eve was tired, but she was determined she would make an evening dinner that would please Cuthbert. After dinner, they relaxed in small chair out on the veranda. It was cold but special. Eve looked up to the sky and was amazed with the millions and millions of stars. Eve felt happy, and Eve generally liked Cuthbert. Then she thought, *What a shame, tomorrow I'm going to murder you.* Then out loud. "What a shame . . ."

Cuthbert replied, slightly lazily, half yawning, "What?"

"Never mind. An old lady."

"You're not an old lady. I'd like to see my mum do as much as you did today."

Once again, she thought, *Yes, you are quite a good boy, but what has to be done will be done.*

Morning came, and they were off. Eve had carefully prepared Cuthbert's favourite tomato soup.

Eve packed it away when she knew later it would be required. They sail out of the harbour into the gulf, such a windless bright day. After they had cleared the entrance to the harbour and were into the gulf, she brought out her soup heavily laced with sleeping pills. Cuthbert drank it greedily, gulping it down, wiping his face with his sleeve.

"My goodness, Eve, that's the best tomato soup I've ever tasted! Would you give the recipe to Grace?"

"Of course!"

Cuthbert was starting to get drowsy.

"Bit sleepy? Take a rest, Cuthbert."

No sooner had he sat down, he fell asleep. Eve waited for some time to make quite sure he was completely asleep; when she thought he was, she got to work. Eve brought up onto the deck the heavy weights that would send him down into the depths of the ocean. Eve very carefully tied them around his belt, brought a knife out of her pocket, cut his finger, took a handkerchief out of her pocket, smeared the blood on it then smeared it on to the jib, wrapped the knife in the handkerchief, threw the handkerchief and the knife inside it overboard, then rolled him to the side of the yacht, and with one almighty push, she shoved him overboard. Eve stood there watching Cuthbert slowly disappear beneath the waves.

Then once the deed was completed, she knew she had to sail the yacht singlehanded back to Auckland. But halfway back, she jumped overboard then got back into the yacht. This was to show that she after seeing Cuthbert hit by the main jib and fell overboard, she jumped in to try to save him. Eve had thought all this through very carefully.

Once back to the mooring, Eve shouted out to make sure as many boat owners could hear what had happened to her, to them, out in the gulf.

Eve waited for the police to arrive; she gave a very gabbled account of what had happened. Eve felt quite pleased with herself; sailing a yacht singlehanded was by no means easy. Of course, people didn't realise what she had done way out in the middle of the gulf. Everyone thought of her as a hero. The police admired this plucky grandmother and her mastery of the sea and not losing her head. They brought her back to her daughter's house, where she told the upset daughter what had happened. Oh, not the murder bit.

The funeral came in the *Herald Newspaper*. Eve was heralded as a brave grandmother who tried to save her son-in-law from the waves. Cuthbert's parents were upset naturally but hailed Eve as a brave woman. The police inspected the yacht and the jib with blue on it. The police had the blood tested, and it was Cuthbert Downer's. The coast guard was sent out to see if a body was floating in the sea but nothing; Eve had made sure of that by weighing down the body with heavy weights.

The days went to years. Life carried on. Eve got older. Her daughter entered into the business, taking over more and more of the work, eventually realising that her mother Eve needed to retire. She had been to many retirement villages; one stood out as being one of the best. Eve was aware of what her daughter was doing, so these very last rest home, she visited them herself and eventually decided on one. It was near Point Chevalier.

It was Selwyn Village. She had picked an apartment in the main building on the fifth floor with a view of the sea. This, she felt, was where she wanted to end her years.

CHAPTER 5

The tree eventually died, and Martin advised his son probably it would be better if he didn't plant another tree there. Martin, of course, knew Iris was underneath the concrete, and her decomposing body had killed the tree.

Martin's son James grew up to be a handsome lad. He married Ruth, a part Maori; her parents were from Christchurch in the South Island. Ruth presented James with Evelyn later. Ruth became pregnant this time; it was a difficult birth, and James lost his adoring wife Ruth and their son.

Years passed. Martin had moved to Thames to run the bakery shop, leaving his son in Auckland with Evelyn in the family home. Martin worked hard at making bread then became sick, sold the bakery, and moved back to live with his son and granddaughter Evelyn.

James had discussed with his dad that he thought he would be much better moving into a retirement home, seeing as Martin's heart wasn't as good as it used to be, and James felt it was better if his dad moved somewhere with doctor and nurses able to help his dad if he had difficulties; they chose Selwyn Village. Martin chose an apartment on the second floor with an inward view of the gardens.

Eve arose out of bed and thought of sightseeing as this was her third day after moving in over the weekend. *I think I'll go down to breakfast in the main restaurant.*

Eve had a shower, dried, put her makeup on, strolled out of her apartment, and waited for the lift.

Martin had been in the village for some weeks, had made a couple of friends, and one or more ladies found him attractive and vied for his attention.

He had showered, shaved, and dressed. Now he was waiting at the lift; he didn't want to go down by the stairs. The lift arrived. A rather attractive woman was in the lift, so he said good morning to her. "Good morning." He ventured a question. "Been here long?"

"I have been here three days. What about you?"

"A couple of weeks?"

They were busy chatting, not realising the lift had arrived at ground floor, where the restaurant was situated; but its door was closed, and they started going back up.

Eve, realising this, burst out into laughter, then Martin laughed too. The lift went up and back down, but by the time it reached ground floor, Eve was in tears, laughing so much.

Martin found this woman so attractive. Just out of the lift, neither realised the lift's door was closing and trapping part of Eve's dress in the doors; off it went, lifting Eve's dress up then tearing the corner off as it carried on. Eve laughed even more as Martin had hold of her dress, trying to retrieve it before tearing her dress and disappearing.

"Well, I suppose that's one way of meeting . . ."

"My goodness, my dress!"

"I am so sorry, it's my fault, I'll buy you a new dress."

"Certainly not! It was as much my fault as yours. We were talking too much."

"You mean laughing too much."

"There is no such thing as laughing too much. What is your name?"

Eve didn't see anyone else, only this rather charming man. Martin felt he had always known this woman, though they had never met before.

"Martin Chivers, and you?"

"Eve Hutton."

Martin offered Eve his arm. "Can I escort you to breakfast, Mrs Eve Hutton?"

She took it. "You most certainly can, Mr Martin Chivers."

They smiled at each other as Martin escorted Eve in to the restaurant.

Whilst all this was going on, Olive Reader had been watching them. Olive snarled at the two new people; she had decided she didn't like neither. Olive was a widow of 40 years; she had been married to Albert Reader, a kind-hearted man. They had a happy but short marriage; no children. Olive didn't like the idea of a baby messing about with her slim body. Living on her own had made her greedy and selfish, never ever thinking of other human, just herself.

Here was Olive, she had been in this hideous village for some time now. Olive hated where she lived, hated her neighbours and all these fools. When she saw the two new ones laughing, it turned her stomach.

Eve and Martin selected a table near the window. Martin pulled the chair out for Eve to sit on it.

"Thank you, Martin!"

He inclined his head and sat opposite her. The other women in the restaurant looked daggers at the new woman. They had selected their food from the kitchen entrance, then moved along to collect orange juice and coffee, then Martin paid for them at the cashier and sat down again. They chatted as they ate and drank.

"Eve, what made you decide to come here?"

Eve explained about her business and why her daughter felt she should retire from work and live somewhere, where Grace felt Eve was going to be looked after. "Martin, what about you?"

Martin said very much the same apart from the fact that his son James was very concerned of Martin's heart problem. Martin had a slight problem with his heart a year ago and thought nothing of it, but James was concerned. The more they chatted, the more Eve found this interesting man so fascinating. Martin couldn't believe he had met such a charming and interesting woman.

They finished breakfast then took a walk around the village, stopping here and there as they chatted and walked.

The following months saw Eve's and Martin's families meet and get on very well to the extent when it was Eve's 70th birthday, Grace asked James if he would help her organise her mother's birthday party. They had asked the management if they could hold the party in the restaurant, and they were more than happy for them to do so, only asking how many guests would be there. Grace informed them there would be about 50 guests attending, quite a number of workers in the factories who knew and respected Eve and relatives from her first and her second marriages.

James had asked if he could also bring a very old aunt. James told Grace this aunt had known his father Martin since his first marriage. James wanted Aunt Dotty to meet Eve. He had seen how his father was when he was with Eve, and he needed Dotty to see what she thought of her. Apart from all sorts of goodies for the party, Grace had asked the kitchen to put aside three cartons of ice creams and a box of ice lollies for the six children who would be there, including Grace's son Giles and James's daughter Evelyn. Everything was going to plan; the adults were getting on so very well. Dotty met and liked Eve; the children ran here and there; Evelyn always making sure she kept Giles in her view as she quite liked this silly but nice boy. The party was getting ready for the fruits and ice cream.

Fanny Drew, the cook, and Beth Saunders were bringing the fruit cocktail displayed in a large bowl. Fanny had instructed Beth to start bringing the ice cream and ice lollies out.

In the kitchen was a very large standing freezer. Beth opened the lid up and propped it open with her elbow as she looked for the ice cream and lollies. No matter where she looked, she could not find the ice cream or the lollies. Beth had pulled nearly everything out of the freezer. Fanny was getting a bit bothered with Beth as she hadn't even brought out not even one box of ice cream.

Fanny left the party and the guests to find out what was holding Beth up; when she got to the kitchen, Beth was surrounded with all sorts of frozen goods.

"What's keeping you, Beth?"

"Mrs Drew, I can't find any ice cream or lollies?"

"I told you last week to order them. So you forgot?"

Fanny was becoming very cross with her assistant, though Beth was always very trust worthy and very good at her work. Fanny had never had to be cross with her ever, and Fanny was surprised with Beth's slip-up. Beth replied to her boss, explaining she had ordered the items. "I did."

"Where are they?"

Beth was now waving her hands and spluttering her next statement as she put her hands on her hips. "I don't know."

"What on earth do you mean?"

"They are not here."

Both women lent up against the wall in the kitchen and stood with their mouths open.

"What are we going to do, Mrs Drew?"

Fanny went to her handbag next to her coat, drew out her purse, sorted out a couple of notes, and gave it to Beth. "Go up to the dairy on Point Chevalier road and get what you can, Beth. I'll stall them in the meantime."

Just before Beth left, Fanny exclaimed in a loud voice, "Beth, I know what happened! That greedy old cow Olive, she's been in my kitchen during the night and slowly pinched all the stuff. That woman gets on my wick. Never mind. Sorry I thought it was your fault."

"That's okay, Mrs Drew."

Fanny let Beth go, and she turned her back to explain to the partygoers that there would be a slight wait for the ice cream and lollies. Fanny had a word with Grace to inform her of what had happened, why and how. James had realised something wasn't quite right, so he asked Grace what the problem was. Grace told him the whole story. Eventually, Martin and Eve found out. The party went off well, so Eve and Martin didn't think of it as a problem.

The next few days there was gossip about Eve's birthday party and where had the ice cream and lollies gone. Most of the villagers knew, of course, who the culprit was. Olive was in the habit of stealing food from the kitchen; nobody had actually found her stealing, yet Fanny and her assistant Beth knew full well who stole from the kitchen. Fanny was positive Olive had been slowly stealing since the ice cream and lollies were delivered and laid into the freezer. Nobody liked Olive. She talked behind people's backs, made trouble by repeating gossip, deliberately caused argument between friends. Everyone agreed Olive was a nasty woman.

One morning near midday Eve and Martin had their morning walk and sat on the wooden bench under a massive lime tree set in the middle of the gardens just outside the main entrance to the apartment. They were just on the point of moving into the reception then onto the restaurant to the right of the office desk.

Josie sat next to Martin on the bench.

"Lovely day?"

As Eve and Martin were brought out of a sort of dreaminess, Josie stretched her legs.

"Both of you haven't been here long, have you?"

They replied, "Not long.?"

Eve smiled at how Martin replied as well as she did. They had reached a strange unsaid understanding, almost as if each of them knew what the other was thinking or about to say. Martin laid his hand on Eve's hand; she looked up into his eyes. They were completely unaware of Josie sitting and talking to them. Then they looked at Josie and started listening to her.

"You have to be careful with that woman."

Eve asked, "Who?"

"Olive, that woman that stole your ice creams and lollies!"

Josie carried on as if Eve and Martin knew all about Olive's nastiness, not only to them but also to everyone in the village; how Olive made trouble and stole. Everyone knew not to leave valuables out in the open because Olive would pick them up and steal them.

"Someone should put that old bagwash down."

Eve looked at Martin, and an unsaid thought went between them; he smiled, and Eve smiled back.

Over the next few days, they slowly told each other their history in detail. They understood why they had to do what they did, which was murder people they felt were a nuisance to society. In fact, they felt quite justified murdering some people. It was a sort of cleansing of humanity. Whilst walking along the beach, Eve brought up the case of Olive. "Olive causes so much upset."

"Yes, Eve."

"We really should deal with her, Martin."

"I agree wholeheartedly, Eve."

"Shall we start planning?"

Martin linked his arm in hers. "High time, my lady."

Eve nestled closer to him; he turned to face, her pulling a stray curl away from her face, then oh so very lightly kissed Eve. Then they parted; he smiled at her, and she smiled back. They saw eye to eye.

The next few days in Eve's apartment, it was a hive of industry. They thought of one possibility then another, finally settling on what they felt would be the perfect crime. They selected an evening when everyone would be watching *Coronation Street* on the TV.

First step—Eve had made some pumpkin soup for Olive and, naturally, laced it with sleeping pills. She had popped around to see Olive in her apartment, just one floor down from hers.

Eve knocked on the door. Olive opened it.

"I thought it was high time we meet. I'm Eve. I've brought you a bowl of soup."

"That's kind, Eve." Olive ushered Eve into her apartment, asked her to sit down, and slowly drank the piping-hot soup. The flavour was so nice, she felt cosy warm; the fluid seemed to go to every extremity of her body. "This is very nice, Eve."

As Olive had a big yarn and put the soup down onto the table, the two ladies chatted for some time . Then Olive quaffed the rest of the soup. Lying back into her armchair, she felt so sleepy. Olive couldn't keep her eyes open 'til at last she shut them. Eve shook her to make sure she was in a deep sleep. Then Eve left her, leaving the door ajar, going to Martin's apartment; he was already waiting for Eve. As soon as she got into his apartment, they turned to go back up to Olive's.

When Martin had moved in, his son James had insisted he take his collapsible wheelchair with him just in case he might need it. Martin wheeled the wheelchair up to Olive's apartment. Eve shut the door. They picked up Olive's body, put it in to the wheelchair, and Martin wheeled it to the lift. In the meantime, Eve had gone down the staircase to the ground floor, got into the waiting lift, pressed Olive's floor, the doors opened, and Martin wheeled Olive in. Once on the ground floor, he wheeled the wheelchair to the kitchen. Finally stopping at the freezer, Eve put one light on in the kitchen and opened the lid of the freezer and propping it up with a large bag of frozen peas. They picked up Olive, slid her into the freezer; only her feet were poking out of the freezer.

"You know, Martin, I have an idea . . ."

As Eve spoke, she leant into the freezer, picked up a couple of iced lollies, and put them into Olive's now-cold hands, and pressed hard on her fingers to close them around the lollies, then Martin started to push Olive's feet into the freezer. But one just would not go in.

"Push, Eve."

"I'm pushing."

Then Eve got the giggles. Martin started sniggering. Then suddenly, they heard a noise. Someone was coming down the stairs. Martin put his finger to his lips and finally pushed Olive's foot into the freezer. Eve and Martin hid around the back of the freezer with the bag of frozen peas in Eve's hand. They waited. Then Greta Barnstable, head of the main office, was doing her regular rounds of the building before she went home for the night. Greta saw that Mrs Drew must have left the light on in her kitchen. She turned it off. Greta hesitated for a few moments, coking her head to one side as if she had heard something. Then she shrugged and left.

"Phew! That was close. I wonder if she saw us, Martin."

"No. I don't think so, Eve."

"We might need to deal with her too."

"Yes, Eve. Come on, let's go."

They very quietly left the kitchen, took the lift to Eve's floor, opened her door, walked in, and flung themselves onto the settee next to the windows. Eve cuddled up to Martin; he put his arm around her.

"Eve?"

"Yes, Martin?" She snuggled even closer to him.

"Eve, I never thought I would find someone like me."

"Me too!" She propped herself on one elbow, gazing at Martin.

"We are lucky."

"Yes, we are, Eve."

She leant over and kissed Martin on the cheek. "I have at last found my soulmate, Martin."

"And I, you."

They fell asleep in each other's arms.

CHAPTER 6

The sun's rays flitted across the sleeping lovers. It danced across their upturned faces across their eyelids. Eventually, the sun played games running along the wall, dancing through the cups and saucers in the kitchen, then alighting back onto the sleeping entangled sweetness of first love.

Eve woke. Was this a dream, or was this real? The soulmate she had always dreamt of was him. Was Martin her lost soul? Martin woke up, her head was on his shoulder; Eve smiled at him.

"Where do we go from here, my love?"

Eve repeated his words. "Where do we go from here, my love?"

"I said it first, Eve."

"Yes, Martin, you did!"

"Well, Eve?"

Eve put her hand behind his head, brought his head and lips to hers; they kissed.

"This is forever, Martin."

"Mrs Eve Hutton . . ."

"Yes . . ."

"I love you!"

"Mr Martin Chivers . . ."

"Yes, Eve?"

"I love you!"

They sank into each other's arms, not wishing to move, least the spell of first love broke.

The full sun shone on them, displaying complete happiness.

Had these two humans murdered an old woman last night? The answer is yes. Now they had the problem of Greta Barnstable. Had she seen them? Had Greta seen them put Olive Reader into the freezer? Whether Greta had or not, they knew they couldn't take that risk. So Greta Barnstable had to be dealt with. After breakfast, they settled down to discuss what should be done with her. Greta had to be silenced and as soon as possible. Martin told Eve that Greta every morning went down to the beach to swim. Maybe she could accidentally drown. How could they do it without being at the beach? Something had to happen before she got to the beach, something that would rend her suddenly unconscious swimming in the sea and drown.

Beth was waiting outside the main doors, waiting for Fanny to arrive as she had the keys to get in.

Leaning up against the glass doors, watching the cars coming in and out, some visitors parking in the car park opposite the main building, Beth was musing, thinking of her two-week off. Beth only had a few weeks to go. She had booked a holiday on the Gold Coast with her best friend Lynda. She was busily daydreaming of lying on the sand, sunbathing, when Fanny turned up.

"Morning, Mrs Drew."

"Morning, Beth."

Fanny hurriedly unlocked the glass sliding door. As the doors opened, Fanny and Beth walked towards the kitchen. Then Fanny stopped just by two armchair in the foyer. Fanny needed to discuss the morning's work. Fanny had a menu in mind and wanted to discuss it with Beth.

Both women settled themselves into the armchairs. Fanny brought out a list of food, going from one item to the next.

"I want you to go to the freezer and get a large leg of lamb. Just defrost it in a large bowl. I don't want any water on the surfaces like last lime when I got you to defrost that pork last week."

"Yes! I am sorry about last week."

Fanny replied in a sort of sigh.

"Yes!"

"Well, let's get going. Time waits for no man."

Fanny brought some vegetables out so that she could prepare them then get Beth cracking. Beth hung her coat up on the hanger next to Fanny's coat, left her handbag on the ledge, and walked to the large freezer. As she got to the freezer, she yarned and rubbed her eyes, opened the lid to the freezer, looked up at the clock to see the time, at the same time felt into the freezer; she knew where she would locate the leg of lamb. Beth felt something odd. It felt like a hand half yarning; she looked at what she had grasped. It was a human hand then an arm and clothing all at once. Beth realised what it was: It was a frozen body clutching two ice lollies in one hand. Beth gave out an almighty scream, shot back as if bitten by a snake. Beth carried on screaming and shaking her hands. Fanny looked up as Beth started screaming; she pushed passed Beth to look into the freezer and fainted. The office girl came running from her desk when she heard the screaming; two old ladies also ran into the kitchen. All four of them found Fanny passed out on the floor, and Beth sat on the floor wailing. Dolores, the office girl, stepped over

Fanny lying on the floor to look at what was in the freezer and promptly screamed. Violet took hold of her friend Wendy to also look into the freezer on seeing the gruesome sight of the body. Wendy went to reach and was sick on the floor. Violet just stared at the frozen body in the freezer.

After Dolores recovered enough, she went back to her office and phoned the police. They came quite promptly, and after interviewing some of the villagers who knew Olive, the detective came to the idea that Olive that night had gone down to the freezer and had reached into it to get some ice cream and fell in and was trapped. It was common knowledge that Olive, being so greedy, had simply slip into the freezer and froze to death.

In the meantime, Eve and Martin's plans were now taking shape after deciding what poison they would use and how and where to administer it. To start the plan rolling, Eve made an appointment with the doctor. Eve took Martin with her. He sat outside, waiting for her. She went into the doctors surgery and complained of constipation; the doctor gave her a prescription to take to the pharmacy.

Eve and Martin walked to get her drugs from the pharmacist.

Whilst inside, waiting for the pharmacist to make up the script, Martin asked the young girl behind the counter to help him find a suitable hair shampoo for dandruff, knowing it was far enough away from the medicines behind the counter, so that it gave Eve plenty of time to locate what she wanted. That was digoxin. Eve knew it was for the heart in small doses. Some weeks before, she had gone to the pharmacy for nail polish so that she could locate the digoxin she wanted. So Eve knew exactly where to find a small syringe and the digoxin. As soon as Eve had picked up what she wanted, she moved over to where Martin and the assistant were. Martin then knew Eve had what she wanted.

The next morning Martin caught a wasp and killed it. Eve put it next to the syringe in her pocket. Then around about 11, when Greta came out to walk to the beach, Eve was waiting for her. Eve said it was such a nice morning for a small walk. Both ladies chatted as they walked down the steps and path down to the changing shed one level up from the beach.

"Eve, I'm just going to change. I won't be long."

"Greta, is there a toilet in there?"

"Yes."

"Thank goodness for that."

Greta went inside and pointed to where the toilet was then started to undress. Eve flushed the toilet, opened the door, then Eve slapped Greta on the back.

"Ouch!"

"Got him, that wasp," jabbing the syringe and giving Greta a lethal dose of the poison, opening up her hand to show Greta the wasp. "Look, I got him! Are you okay?"

"Gosh, that really stung."

"Look, Greta, it's one of those German wasps. You're lucky I got him. They sting then carry on stinging you."

Once again, Eve made sure Greta was fine. Greta started putting her clothes back on.

"I'm going back to the office to clean the wound."

"Greta, if you carry on and go into the sea, it'll clean it."

"Really?"

"Oh yes."

Greta seemed a bit surprised but slowly removed what clothing she had on and put her swimsuit on. "Thank you, Eve." And she promptly left the changing shed and ran down to the beach.

Eve followed.

"I'll sit here and take care of your valuables as you swim."

Greta didn't wait to reply to Eve but dashed into the sea and dived in. Greta was a strong swimmer; at school, she was in the school swimming team and won a couple of cups for her swimming. So as usual, she swam strongly out into the surging waves; the sea was warm. Once she felt she was out far enough and the wasp sting didn't seem as bad as at first, she wallowed in the salty water, allowing the waves to buff her about. Greta did breast strokes until she became tried.

All this time, Eve sat on a metal seat facing the sea, watching Greta swim. The poison seemed to be taking quite some time to react. Still, Eve watched; sooner or later, it would work.

Greta couldn't lift her head out of the water, so Greta rolled over on her back. Then very slowly, her extremities started to cramp, not only her feet but her whole body. Greta tried to lift her hand out of the water but couldn't lift it out. Her heart was beating loudly in her ear. Greta thought, *Oh my god, I'm having a heart attack!*

Then she started to panic. Greta tried to scream, but nothing came out; all Greta did was take large gulps of seawater, coughing and spluttering. Greta tried to splash, make some noise, anything. Greta slowly started to sink into the sea, lower and lower. Greta could see the sandy bottom of the sea. Fish were swimming up to her to investigate her body. Slowly, her lungs were filling with seawater, and Greta was drowning, then nothing.

Eve suddenly could not see Greta in the sea. Couples walked along the beach, passing a supposed sleeping Eve, waiting for her friend to come back to shore. Eve looked at her watch; she had been there for an hour. Eve got up and walked to the sea edge, shielding her eyes with her right hand, looking for Greta but of course, knowing she had drowned some time ago.

Eve asked a man swimming in the sea had he seen a woman. He said no. Eve looked upset. "Please help me! My friend has been out in the sea for such a long time. I can't see her at all."

The man responded and dived out to swim to see if he could see anything under the sea, but he couldn't and came back to Eve. "There is nothing out there. I can't see a thing."

Eve seemed upset. "Oh my goodness, Greta should be back by now."

By now, quite a large gathering of people was around Eve. One young boy said he would get his bicycle and get the police, which he did.

Eventually, the police arrived, took by now the crying Eve back to the village. Martin kept completely out of the way in his apartment. A number of Eve's acquaintances helped her in her apartment to settle down with sweet cups of tea then leaving Eve to sleep. Mary stayed with Eve as she slept.

Later in the evening, Eve told Mary that she was feeling a bit better and that Mary should go to grab a bite to eat.

"I'll be fine, Mary, really."

"So long as you're sure, Eve."

"Go. I'll be okay."

When Eve was sure that Mary had gone to get some food, she made her way to Martin's apartment; she knocked on the door, and he opened it. Once inside, he asked her, "Are you all right, Eve?"

Eve nodded. "Everything went to our plan."

He took her hand and led her to his window. "You are such a clever woman."

"The police are going to search the beach."

Eve laid her head on his shoulders, and they held hands, looking out to the vista of the tropical plants in the garden.

Towards the evening, the police divers located Greta's body and brought it back to the beach.

CHAPTER 7

A week passed, and by that time, the police had found that Greta Barnstable had drowned, and there were no extenuating circumstances.

Life went on in the village. The villagers noted that Eve and Martin were always together and were equally interested in general complaints that the villagers had, like Mrs Greenaway's cat, Patch, constantly urinating in Mr Pott's small garden just outside his unit. The cat was found, and it seemed it had eaten poison. Naturally, Mrs Greenaway was so upset; a week later, she had to report to the doctor with a nasty upset stomach.

Joey, the yellow-crested cockatoo, was driving Rose Patterson crazy with its constant screeches and rude language. Rose asked Eve to see and hear what the problem was. Both ladies turned the corner of Rose's unit; there, in the garden, Sydney had lifted Joey out in the air. As soon as Joey saw Rose, he screeched out to Rose in a greeting, "Piss off! Piss off!" Joey kept on until Rose and Eve disappeared inside Rose's unit.

"You can see what I mean—filthy language, I can't stand it!"

"Have you explained to Sydney about your problem?"

"Yes!"

"What's the problem, Rose?"

"He laughs at me."

"I'll have a word with him."

"Would you, Eve? That damn bird is upsetting me."

Eve did no more than go straight next door to talk to Sidney South. Eve knocked on the door; a small old man came to the door. "I suppose you want to talk to me about Joey, Mrs Hutton."

"Yes, I do."

As soon as Eve got inside the door and was ushered to a seat near Joey, the bird started to screech at Eve, "Piss off! Piss off!" and kept going.

Sydney walked over to where Joey was perched, and Sydney lifted him onto his outstretched hand and started stroking him. "Who's a good boy?"

Joey shouted back, "Joey! Joey!" And the bird's head kept jerking from side to side.

"See, he's a sweet bird. Go on, stroke him."

Eve started to stroke the head of the bird. And the bird started reciting that he was a pretty boy.

"He is a lovely bird. Is there any way you can come to an agreement with Rose?"

"I have never tried."

"Is it okay if I go next door and bring her over?"

"Certainly."

Eve went next door to Rose and brought her to Sydney's unit. Rose came in rather gingerly and sat on the settee. Sydney brought Joey over to her and suggested she stroke him, which she did, then Joey again said what a pretty boy he was. Eve sat still watching Rose and the bird the spoke up. "What do you think Rose?" It seemed that Rose was getting on very well with Joey. Eve had another idea. "Rose, what if you try to teach Joey some nice words?"

Rose thought for some time then replied to Eve and Sydney, "If it's all right with you, I could."

"What do you think, Sydney?"

"I'm game if you are, Rose."

Eve felt pleased with herself; she had defused a disagreement. Now Rose agreed to teach the bird nicer words, and Rose wouldn't make any more fuss about Joey telling her to piss off.

Eve felt happy that she had sorted the problem out. When Eve got back to the apartment where Martin was sat fast asleep in the armchair, Eve very quietly crept in and sat in her armchair, saying to herself that she would tell Martin about Joey but fell asleep.

Other smaller incidentals had to be dealt with. Eve and Martin were kept very busy helping their fellow villagers out, making sure that the village itself ran smoothly. James and Grace had been seeing quite a lot of each other to the point that Evelyn, James's daughter, and Giles, Grace's son, felt it was high time they had a talk to their grandparents. They had taken the day off school and taken the trolley bus to the village. There were their grandparents, sitting in the lounge with Edna Smith, grumbling about her next-door neighbour Wallace Grant. "He has his music on so loud I can't hear my television program. Always, when I turn on *Coronation Street*, there goes his music!"

Yesterday Wallace had complained about Edna putting her TV on just at the same time he wanted to listen to the concert program.

Eve and Martin had decided that Edna and Wallace were as bad as each other, so they needed to come up with a plan that would deal with them.

"Edna, Eve and I have taken notes, and we will get back to you."

Edna was pleased that Eve and Martin listened to her problem because whenever problems arose in the village, after Eve and Martin had been consulted, somehow the problems just vanished. Edna and her husband Wallace went back to watching television.

Eve could now concern herself with the grandchildren. "How's my favourite grandchildren?"

Giles replied to his grandmother, "Nana, fine but—"

"Tell me, what's the problem?" Eve cupped Giles's chin in her hand. "Well, my naughty one, tell your Nana."

Martin joined in. "What's up, lad?" The he looked towards Eve.

Eve just shrugged. "So far, my dear, our naughty bees haven"t told me anything.."

They could see that Evelyn and Giles looked very serious. And the asked their grand rents if they could go somewhere private. Martin realised this was important, so he suggested they go out ide and sit on one of the metal seat' in the garden. Once they had arrived at the garden, all four selected a garden seat where they could all sit together and have some privacy.

"I think you two children had better tell Eve and myself what you're concerned about."

All four sat there for some time then Evelyn spoke up, speaking in a clinical way. "It has come to our attention . . .," pointing to Giles.

Giles took over from Evelyn. "What Evelyn and I are trying to say . . ."

"We have noticed that our parents have been seeing a lot of each other."

"Evelyn and I are very concerned, and we felt you should be told."

Eve started to snigger but very quickly got her handkerchief out and put it over her mouth to prevent the children hearing her. At the same time, she looked across at Martin who was equally trying so hard to keep a straight face. They managed to stop themselves from embarrassing the children.

Evelyn could see that their grandparents were trying so hard to be serious, and she felt that they were not realising the gravity of what she and Giles were concerned about.

"Nana, it's no laughing matter!"

Eve replied, "Evelyn and Giles, your parents are adults. Don't you think they can make their own minds up regarding each other?"

Giles replied but rather sheepishly, "Well, yes. I suppose?"

She carried on, trying to help them understand. "They may well like each other a lot and feel the need to be with each other to see if they want to go any further."

Eve thought she had hit the nail on the head this time and was shocked with the next remark from Giles. "Nana, they are like you two."

Martin quickly replied, "Us."

"Yes, Granddad."

Evelyn was busy nodding to her grandson Giles. Martin and Eve looked at each other; they had their mouths open.

"Evelyn and I can see you love each other."

Both grandparents nodded.

A long silence. Eve could hear the birds in the trees. Martin heard Fanny in the kitchen finishing up lunch; she had dropped a pan on the floor and shouted at Beth to help her clear it up.

Both children folded their arms, waiting for a response from their grandparents, but still silence.

Eve eventually spoke. "So what do we do? What do you two think we should do?"

Evelyn replied, "Why don't you and Grandad get married?"

The children had started out by making Eve and Martin understand their parents and their feelings for each other.

Evelyn spoke. "Mum and Dad want to get married as well."

They hugged and kissed their grandparents and left, leaving Eve and Martin.

Martin looked at her. Eve looked at him. The children were busy walking out of the garden. Eve clasped Martin's hand. "Have we been far too busy with other people's problems that we have not realised what's happening with us?"

"I think we have, my dear." Martin told Eve how he felt and that being with her was the best thing that had ever happened to him.

Eve felt exactly the same. They held each other's hands and declared their love for each other. They realised, out of the whole world, they had found a soulmate. Martin got down on one knee.

"Get up, Martin. If you are going to ask me to marry you, the answer is yes!"

"Haven't asked you yet."

"But you are going to!"

"Yes. Eve, I love you."

"And, Martin, I love you."

Eve tried to help Martin up back onto the seat, it wasn't so easy, but eventually, he was sat next to her. They kissed, and the world stood still just for one second; one moment in time, two elderly people had found each other. Even though they were murderers and had done some very wicked things, they had truly fallen madly in love, something neither had ever felt before.

A few days later, they told their son and daughter and, naturally, their grandchildren.

Eve and Martin wasted no time. Martin moved into Eve's apartment and informed the management of their decision. They, in turn, found a new occupant for his apartment.

So now it was just a matter of when were they going to get married; they chose Valentine's Day, Eve's birthday, for the ceremony, and it would take place in the small church in the village.

CHAPTER 8

Once all the family knew of Eve and Martin's wedding, they all wanted to help; cousin Dotty from Thames said she would deal with the flowers, first of all, to decorate the church and Eve's bouquet and the bridesmaids, who were Evelyn and Grace. James booked the church inside Selwyn village for 14 February, Eve's birthday and Valentine's Day. Dotty had spoken to Eve over her favourite colour, which was violet or mauve. Accompanied by Dotty, Eve's daughter Grace, James's daughter Evelyn, and a dear friend from the village Polly, Eve knew a very good dressmaker in Avondale, Hilton Key, and Tex, his assistant. Eve had made an appointment for midday Tuesday. Eve and her companions opened Hilton's door. Hilton was behind the counter. Eve spoke to Hilton. "We are right on time, Hilton."

"First of all, do call me Paris, and this is my assistant and boyfriend Tex."

Paris was quite effeminate, short, and slim, with a shock of red hair; whereas, Tex was quite the opposite, tall and broad. Grace thought he looked like a prize fighter more than a dressmaker. But then when he spoke, he had a very high voice, and the two of them looked like one big tall fairy and one ginger fairy. Both flapped around the shop.

"Darling, you look just darling. Doesn't she, Tex?"

"Yes, Paris. What colour was madam thinking of?"

Paris very quickly butted in. "White!"

"Paris, can't you see Eve is not white?"

"Tex, dear, what do you think?"

"Paris, dear, usually, the bride wears white. But don't you think she would look darling in, say, pink?"

At this point, Paris and Tex got into a sort of heavy discussion about the pros and cons of wedding attire, leaving the ladies to giggle. Evelyn and Polly had their hands over their mouths, trying to stop themselves from laughing out loud. Grace and Eve were trying without success to bring some order in to the whole affair, which wasn't happening at all, and eventually gave up. Then from out of the back of the main shop came a very skinny old woman; she stood for some time as if listening for the right moment to step in. She stood with her hands on her hips, surveying the discord, then suddenly, without warning, in a quiet voice, said, "Stop this."

Nothing happened; the disagreement was carrying on as if she wasn't there. Then she came around the side of the counter, this time raising her voice so that the two men stopped in mid-discussion and the four women looked to her. "I said stop."

Complete silence—a pin could be heard dropping. Paris looked at Tex. Tex looked at the old lady.

"Boys, that's enough."

All eyes were on the old lady.

"I'm the owner and Hilton's mother."

Still silence. Grace cleared her throat and spoke. "Hello, Mrs Key."

"Around here, I'm called the boss." She lifted one hand from her hip to sweep around the shop, alighting on her son and Tex. "And these two are my boys. Now that's been sorted out, you two will get cracking and sorting out this lady's wedding dress colour." She turned around went back the way she had come and disappeared out of sight.

This time Paris asked Eve what colour she would like. Eve told him violet was her favourite colour.

He instructed Tex to do the measurement of the bridesmaids, and he looked after Eve. No mention of Paris's mother or her Christian name was made. Tex and Paris just referred to her as the boss.

After Paris and Tex had finished with the measurements, Tex wrote them into a small book then put in in the draw of the counter. The boss came in again, this time smiling. "They are good boys, really." She tousled Paris's hair. "Paris is clever." Then as a second thought, "And Tex."

Tex beamed from ear to ear as if he were a puppy and had just been tickled.

"Now it's up to me to get the boys working. I will let you know when to come back for a fitting."

That was it, finished. A week went by, and Eve got a call from Tex for the ladies to come back for a last-minute fitting the next day around midday again.

All four women got to the dressmaker's at ten to 12. Opening the door, there were Paris and Tex, welcoming them in. Tex spoke first. "Do come in!"

Paris shouted out to his mother out the back, "Boss!"

Eve started wondering if the boss actually had a Christian name at all and was determined to ask either Paris or Tex what her name was at a suitable time.

The dresses were brought in; all, except Polly, went into three cubicles in the workroom to change into their dresses. Once the first woman came out, Polly went in to change. By now, Paris had started rearranging Eve's dress. He flitted around like a fairy flapping his wings when he needed to change direction. He flapped even harder. Tex seemed more matter-of-fact; he dealt with Grace then the two other women, first Polly. The boss was standing to the side then started to deal with Evelyn's dress. All four women were finally dressed and almost finished. The boss spoke to Eve. "Well, what do you think?"

Eve did a small pirouette, looked at herself in the long mirror, patting down the dress starting from her bosoms over and down as far as she could; the other three were looking on excitedly.

"Well?"

"It's—oh! Words can't express what I feel."

The boss beamed from ear to ear. "You're a princess, that's what!"

Like a ballerina, Eve spun around the workroom. "It's beautiful. I can't keep calling you the boss, can I?"

The boss cocked her head like a chicken cocks its head, then almost meekly and fluttering her eyes as she answered, clearing her throat before she spoke, "My name is Annabelle. My husband would call me Belle."

Eve thought Annabelle didn't look like an Annabelle because her hands and fingers were quite large, a working woman's hands; she was short, skinny, with a ruddy complexion—definitely not an Annabelle. Eve replied carefully, "What a pretty name."

"There was a time when I was quite a stunner," Annabelle said, blushing. Then very quickly, the boss face came back. "Er! If you come back in three days' time, I'll have everything ready for you. Oh! And this," Annabelle said, as if she had forgotten, but Eve knew she hadn't.

Annabelle brought out a heavily-embroidered veil, placing it on Eve's head; it fell over her eyes and slightly down the back, not too far. Grace, seeing this and how happy her mother was, brought out a small handkerchief and wiped a tear from her eye. "Mum, you look so beautiful!"

Eve, as if in a trance, spun around. "Do you think Martin will like it?"

"Mum." And she swept her mother into her arms. "You love him, don't you?"

"He's my soulmate."

"I know." And she hugged her mother even more.

Even the boss wiped a tear from her eye. Paris and Tex were tearful and flapped their hands over their faces.

"Oh mi, don't she look the picture, Tex?"

"Yes, love."

As Paris turned to go back inside the workroom, Tex slapped his bottom.

"Oh you!"

Annabelle shrugged. "That's mi boys."

The four women went back to the village, had a cup of tea in Eve and Martin's apartment. Grace addressed Martin, "Martin, are you going to have a stag night?"

"What, me?"

All three women, except Eve, replied, "Yessss."

Eve reacted almost like a young bride and blushed.

"I hadn't really thought about it, Grace." He looked at Eve and walked over to her, taking her hand in his and bringing it up to his lips to kiss. Then bowing very low, he said, "I'm forgetting my age."

Eve very quickly put her hand over his, helping him straighten himself up. "I want you in one piece, Martin."

"Eve, you'll always have me in one piece."

And they kissed like two teenagers.

The ladies went for their fittings, and as before, Paris flapped here and there, Tex seemed more matter-of-fact, and Annabelle pocked her head around the door from the workshop. "Everything fine, Eve?"

"Yes. Wonderful."

As Grace helped her mother and Evelyn gather the dresses up and lay them in the back seat of her Holden estate car, Paris and Tex stood at the opened door to the shop with the boss woman behind. Paris shouted out, "Bye, darlings!"

Tex and Paris waved; the boss woman stood behind her son.

CHAPTER 9

The night before the wedding, Martin was given his instruction for the night. James had organised Martin's stag night. Then Martin would stay with his son and grandson overnight. James had invited Grace's son, Giles; two of the old boys from the village, Jack and Charlie, both were very old but bright old fellows; Dotty's son, Willy; Eddy and Clifford, these last two men were from the Huttons, the family of Eve's second husband; but James wasn't exactly sure whose sons they were.

Once all the men were at James's house, they readied themselves to go to the Three Lamps in Ponsonby. It wasn't that difficult to find; the old hotel, a colonial hotel built in the 1920s or so, was on the corner of Ponsonby and Jervois roads. A large building in front stood a lamp with three lamps on it. The gathering of men sauntered in to the bar. It had been recommended by Eddy and Clifford. Apparently, both men were now working at the factory of the Huttons, and Grace was their boss. They said they came here quite often, just before the bar swill at six o'clock, when all the men in the bars had to place their orders as quickly as they could before the bar closed; hence, it really was a dash to get as many beers down them before the last bell sounded.

They all entered at five o'clock; the bar was blue with stale smoke. Behind the bar were two rather largely-bosomed women pouring out as many jugs of beer as they could. Eddy, a part Maori, informed the other men in the party the names of the women at the bar. "That's Stacy. Take a gander at those tits, boys," pointing to a very busty woman of about 30, with long blond hair and heavily-rouged face. "That's Nancy," he added, pointing to a rather tall woman with black hair but definitely not a woman. "Don't cross Nancy, she'll throw you out as quick as you like."

Charlie turned to Eddy. "Isn't she a he?"

"If you get pissed tonight, you might find out, Charlie. I wouldn't turn your back on her if I were you."

The other men sniggered as if they were teenagers. Willy was telling dirty jokes, making Martin quiver with laughter. Eddy ordered beer for all of them; the woman had very carefully filled a small glass up and put it upside down at the bottom of each glass. Then with the jug, Eddy poured beer into each glass. Martin exclaimed, "What's that?"

"It's called a depth charge!"

"Can Giles manage it? He's just sixteen."

Once again, Eddy replied, "It'll put hair on his chest or take them off!"

Martin tried vainly to shout over the din in the bar of men shouting, laughing, telling rude jokes, carousing with the girls behind the bar.

Eddy assured him that Giles would be able to manage it, and besides, they all considered him a man, except for James and Martin. Both shook their heads.

"If the women find out, they are going to kill us."

Martin looked at his son, and before he could say anything, the boys brought their glasses together, and half the contents were gone, and besides, the noise in the bar made it completely impossible to make themselves heard anyway.

Eventually, Martin felt quite happy, no, drunk; so was his son James. At the sound of the six-o'clock swill, all were happy boys. Eddy seemed hardly affected by consuming so much beer. They all staggered outside, and when the air hit them, it kind of screwed into their brains. All piled into Eddy's truck. He drove them back to James's house. Martin, James, and Giles collapsed into their beds; the others stayed in the lounge, carrying on drinking and playing cards for the rest of the night.

Early in the morning, Grace and Evelyn went over to the dress shop to collect the dresses. The ladies had got themselves ready earlier than the men and were in Eve and Martin's apartment when James came to pick up his dad. James left with his father Jack. Charlie were in the car with Eddie driving and Willy sitting next to Eddie. Eve opened the window to wave to Martin; he never saw her. Shutting the window, Eve mentioned to Grace that she was hoping James would keep Martin out of trouble. As she stated, "Grace, James will keep Martin safe, won't he?"

"Mum, I'm sure he will."

"Because I'm marrying that man of mine tomorrow."

"James is very sensible."

What Eve didn't see was that Grace had her hands behind her back with her fingers crossed. Grace took her mother by the hand.

"Are we ready, ladies?"

All responded with a yes.

Evelyn and Stacy, her friend from school, picked up her grandmother's shawl. Grace had instructed Evelyn to bring something warm for her mother just in case she got cold. The other two ladies was Maureen, who was Eve and Martin's next-door neighbour, and Edith. Maureen was last out of the apartment. Grace turned back to address Maureen. "Maureen?"

"Yes, Grace?"

"Make sure the door is pulled shut. Sometimes the lock at the back jumps out."

"Done it."

"Right. We are off, ladies."

The laughing happy band of women made their way to the lift and downstairs to the car park.

Half got into Grace's Holden, and Maureen had a Hillman Imp. The cars drove up to Point Chevalier shops, where there was a very nice small cafe and bar. All seven ladies filed into the cafe. The owner, Gen-na Stonner, had been contacted by Grace a week ago to book a table, notifying Gen-na that it was a girls' night before her mother was married. Gen-na asked Freda to be their waitress for the night. Grace had brought around to the cafe some bottles of wine for the night, with the idea that the waitress brought them out when and if the party of ladies wanted them. Maureen brought out a white tea cloth and placed it on Eve's head, making it look like a veil. Edith had already fixed some fairy wings on Eve. Eve, all this time, was in fits of laughter. Evelyn and Stacy wound some sprigs of flowers into the tea towel veil.

Grace had arranged with Gen-na to do a set dinner; she knew what sorts of food her mother liked. Evelyn and Stacy didn't mind whatever they eat; neither did Polly, Maureen, and Edith.

The meal started with cubes of chicken on a stick grilled with a peanut sauce and a very small salad of mixed lettuce and grated carrots with a light French dressing.

Then a gurnard fillet in bread crumbs salad dressing with tomatoes cut to look like a rose.

Next was a chicken breast rolled in bacon hassle back potatoes finger length carrots in a spicy sauce. To finish, a cheesecake Grace had made and brought it to the cafe with the decorations. The cheesecake was topped with a mix of kiwi fruit and strawberries and lashings of cream.

Gen-na brought the cheesecake out with a bit of theatrics. She had planted a large relight-able candle. There were gasps of delight around the cafe. Then Gen-na placed it in front of Eve.

"It's my wedding and my birthday. I had better blow it out."

Eve took one big breath then blew hard. The candle went out. Then to much laughter, the candle started to relight.

"Now what?"

"You'll have to blow it out again, Mum."

"You're a cruel daughter."

Grace gave her mother a big kiss. "I get it all from you, Mother."

"I hope not everything, Grace."

Grace looked at her mother, remembering all those years back when Cuthbert was alive, though Grace's mother never knew that her daughter had known all along that her mother had done what she had done to Cuthbert only for her. Grace was horrified at first when she had put two and two together. But in hindsight, she knew that she and Eve would not be here unless her mother hadn't have drowned Cuthbert. Grace wouldn't have met James. Strangely, James had always suspected his father Martin of doing the same to his mother and his foster mother. So for Grace, this point in time was when their families were going to be joined for love but because of murder.

"Come on, Mum, blow it out."

"No, Grace, Mother has a much better idea." Eve reached down to her handbag, took out her nail scissors, and snipped the wick off the candle. Everyone in the cafe clapped. "What about that, my daughter?"

"You're smarter than the average bear, mummy darling."

Mother and daughter hugged for the birthday and wedding. Also, Grace hugged her mother for everything Eve had done for her.

The dinner and festivities came to an end, and the party of ladies drove back to the village. Polly, Maureen, and Edith said their good-nights then left for their own homes in the village. Grace, Evelyn, and Stacy stayed with Eve that night, Grace making sure the two girls were happily in bed. Grace stayed with her mother. Grace, taking hold of her mother's hand, lightly squeezed it. Grace looked at her mother. Eve was getting older; wisps of white hair were in amongst the dark hair, and such blue trusting eyes.

"Mum."

"Yes, my darling."

"I know everything."

Eve answered, almost scared of what her daughter might say, "Not everything, Grace." Eve moved a stray lock of hair from Grace's forehead.

"Yes, Mum."

Nothing was explained, but both women knew what the other meant.

"I have never fallen in love, Grace. Then Martin came into my life. Never ever did I ever imagine I would meet my soulmate." As Eve said this, tears ran freely down her face. "I am not a good person. I have done bad things for, I felt, the right reason but still bad."

"Yes, Mum."

"I swear this is the first time I've felt love, and, Grace, it's wonderful but scary too. Martin is my life, my whole being. He dies, I die. I would not wish to live if he were not beside me. Grace, understand me, Martin and I are one individual, we are complete, my love for him is always and ever."

"Oh, Mum."

Eve took her daughter's face in her hands. "When you find that perfect love, nothing else matters." Eve kissed her daughter's forehead. "My daughter, just look at you, I made you."

Both woman held each other for now and forever.

CHAPTER 10

On 14 February, Eve's birthday and their wedding day, Martin looked out of his son's bedroom window to a bright summer morning. He thought back to his long life of mistakes, first his first marriage to Iris. She was a nasty type of woman, bitter, selfish, and, oh, so very cruel. He let her drown. Then there was Jenny; their marriage started out fine, she seemed to be a good choice, but soon she changed into another money-hungry woman and no love in her. Martin killed her in their kitchen then took the body to their new house, only to find that she was still alive, so he had to hit her with a spade then entomb her under cement in the floor of his new home.

Here he was on a new day, a new dawning to his life, his wedding day to the one woman he knew he would be happy with for the rest of his life. Out of all the humans in the world, he had found his soulmate, Eve, a new beginning; all he could see was happiness forever.

The sun's rays danced along the ceiling of their apartment. It ran down the wall, glinting on whatever it passed over, sparkling over Eve's eyes, as if it were fairy dust touching her wedding ring from Steven. Eve opened her eyes, alighting on the ring. Eve looked at it and remembered the day she married Steven, a good man, a kind man. Eve lost their child when she realised, to her horror, that she had accidentally killed Steven. Eve never intended to kill him; it was meant for his sister Brenda. Everything had gone so terribly wrong. He should never have died, but if he hadn't, then Eve would not be here on the eve of her wedding day to marry the man of her dreams. Eve slowly removed Steven's wedding band and put it into the palm of her hand. The sun's rays danced on it. Then Eve placed it in an envelope and placed it into the writing desk.

"Steven, I am so sorry, but if you hadn't have died, then I would never have found Martin. Steven, I love Martin. He is everything to me." Eve shed tears of regret and happiness that electrified her whole body.

There was Allen, her first husband; he was a monster and deserved to die. Grace's husband Cuthbert, he was lazy. Eve had to murder him too. But by the time they had sailed to Great Barrier Island, she could see he wasn't quite so bad a person. Eve had planned the murder, and it had to be carried out for the love of her daughter Grace.

James crept into the bedroom, his sleeping father lay on his side, looking out of the window. James crept around to his side then noticed his father Martin was crying. He bent down to his father. "Dad, what's up?"

"I was just thinking, James."

James sat on the bed, took one of Martin's hands in his. Martin's hand was cold. Martin wiped the tears from his face with the other hand.

"James, you should never look back on your mistakes. Just forward to a bright horizon."

"You love her, don't you?"

"Yes, my son, we have so little time left. I should have met Eve years ago."

James took his father in his arms, held him, and told his father, "It's your wedding day, Dad. You had better take Mum's wedding ring off."

Martin looked down at his wedding finger; there it was, Jenny's wedding band. He gripped it with his other fingers. It wouldn't budge. He tried in vain to remove it, but try as he may, still, the ring remained where it was.

"It has got to come off, James."

James stood up, started to go out of the bedroom, and turned back to his father. "Dad, it is coming off."

He went into the bathroom, brought the bar of soap out, and gave it to Martin. He rubbed it around the finger and pulled with all his might. Then slowly, the ring popped off. Martin held it up to the sun; a ray of light hit it, turning the gold to a burning fire. Martin dropped it as if it were lava burning into his fingers. The ring lay on the bed. He looked at it as if he expected it to catch the sheets on fire. Martin picked it up, put it into the palm of his hand, and closed his fingers around it, then quickly placed it into a draw in the small cabinet next to the bed.

"James, don't let me forget it. If I do, put it into an envelope for me."

James nodded to his father.

After breakfast, Giles, Uncle Willy, and Martin went for a short walk up to the summit of One Tree Hill with Wolfe, Evelyn's wire-haired pointer dog. They all scrambled over volcanic boulders. The dog ran here and there, smelling out rabbits that had burrowed in amongst the shards of earth rubble and boulders spewed up from the volcano's throat and left over from the eruption many millions of years ago. Wolfe knew he could smell those damn rabbits; he ran here and there, every so often stopping, wagging his small stomp of a tail, then barking, looking up to James, almost saying to his master, "It's here, master, I've found it for you," tThen suddenly racing off in another direction, barking, wagging his tail.

"olfe ever catch a rabbit, James?"

"You must be joking, Willy. If he ever did catch one, I'm not sure what the silly dog would do with it."

Giles ran after the daft dog, almost as if he too were trying to catch a rabbit. Then just at that moment, one very agile rabbit poked his head out of his burrow and flew for his life; the dog and the young man ran as if their lives depended on catching the running foe.

"James, that dog would make a great hunter. I'd love to take him on my pig hunting just behind Thames. There are quite a lot of Captain Cookers up in the back logs. If you lend him to me some time, I'll swap you for some pig meat."

"Wolfe is Evelyn's dog. I'm not sure if she would agree to it, mate. But ask her."

Eventually, the men and the dog walked back to the house. They all needed to get dressed then to deliver Martin to the church. But before that happened, James took his father aside. He took an envelope out of his pocket.

"Dad, this is for you and Eve."

Martin took the envelope, unsealed it, and brought out a slip of paper with a hotel booking on it. Martin looked at it. "Oh, son, you shouldn't have."

"Dad, this is our wedding present from the family. It's two weeks up at Bay of Islands, staying at the Duke of Wellington at Russell."

Martin hugged his son.

After making coffee, Eve sat looking out at the Waitakeres gazing at the splendour of the trees sweeping down almost to the city.

Evelyn stretched and yawned as she walked into the lounge and sat with a plonk next to Eve, nearly spilling Eve's cup of coffee. Eve instinctively put her hand over the top of the mug.

"Evelyn, be careful!"

"Sorry, Nana." Evelyn put her arm around Eve's shoulders. "This is the day, Nana."

"Yes, my bad imp."

"You know you could pull out. Just think about it, try living in sin with Martin."

Eve responded slightly cross with her granddaughter, "Evelyn, I do not know where you get these ideas from. It's not me, and I bought very much if it would be your dad or grandfather."

Evelyn kissed Eve on the cheek. "It's all the rage, Nan." Then Evelyn started to tease Eve. "Why don't you?"

Eve picked up the tea towel that was over the arm of her armchair and flicked it at Evelyn. "Oh, Evelyn."

Both sniggered.

"Nana better get herself showered and dressed. Otherwise, there will be no wedding."

"See, you don't have to, do you?"

"Evelyn, I can see we are going around in circles. Leave your Nana alone."

The young girl spun around like a ballerina.

"Get yourself dressed, young lady."

With all the commotion going on, it woke the other women. Grace very sleepily came into the lounge, so did Stacy. Rubbing her eyes, Stacy looked out of the window. "You two do make a noise."

"My grandmother is getting married today."

Stacy looked to the sky and made a large sigh and put her hands on her hips. "Evelyn's going to be terrible at school."

"How many time does your grandmother get married, Stacy?"

Grace and Eve ignored the gossiping girls and drank their coffee.

Then it was the time to do makeup and dress. Grace and the girls were dressed. When there was a knock at the door, Eve opened the door. Standing in front of her was a woman of about 30 with a small case and a couple of white sheets. Eve felt a bit taken aback and enquired what the mystery person wanted. "Yes. You are?"

The woman had a very broad smile. Eve noticed she had very white teeth. "Are you Mrs Eve Hutton?" The woman didn't wait for a reply but carried on. "I'm here to do your hair and nails."

The two girls interrupted her. "Eve, it's our present, from us to you. It's a makeover."

Eve put her hands over her mouth and exclaimed, "Oh my goodness! You shouldn't have, girls. Did you know about this, Grace?"

"No, Mum. It was all the girls' idea."

"My name is Jane Owen."

Eve ushered Jane in, and she did no more than open the case to show she had all sorts of combs, scissors, mirrors, gels, and shampoos. Jane sat Eve in one of her kitchen chairs and set to shampoo and set Eve's hair. Whilst Jane did her work, Grace made tea for everyone and opened one of her mother's cake tins and brought out a carrot cake Eve made the day before, carefully cutting a slice for each woman plus her mother Eve.

Eventually, Jane seemed to think she had finished with a few clips of hair that she felt needed to go. Jane stepped back to look at her master piece. "There what do you think of what I have done? Happy?"

Eve took the mirror, looked at her hair from this angle, then that Jane held a mirror behind Eve's head. Eve looked into it, admiring herself. "Jane, that looks good!" Eve turned around to see her granddaughter Evelyn, Stacy, and her daughter Grace beaming from ear to ear. "So I take it you all approve."

"Mum, you look beautiful. The perfect bride!"

"Well, I suppose I had better get married."

Eve thanked Jane, and all four women prepared to take the lift down to the ground floor, where all the office staff were, including the kitchen staff Fanny and Beth.

CHAPTER 11

Martin sat very quietly next to his son James, waiting for his bride-to-be Eve. This was his third marriage, but this time it was for love, understanding, peace, and tranquillity to a true soulmate. In all of Martin's dreams, he never thought he would find a life companion like Eve; she was everything to him. Eve knew his moods and thoughts. He knew she made him complete. They were as one human. A thousand things were going on his head. Martin turned around to see that the small church had filled up with residents from the village, office staff, and his family and Eve's. James nudged his father's elbow. Martin turned to face his son.

"Okay, Dad?"

"No!"

"It will not take long, Dad."

"It's not that so much. I just hate waiting."

Before James could respond to his father, there was a commotion at the door to the church. The organ played a simple tune. Martin's head was a complete jumble; he had no idea what the organist was playing anyway.

"Here Eve comes, Dad."

All Martin could hear was his own heart pounding in his head.

"You had better get up, Dad."

James almost had to push his father to move. Then Martin turned his head; his heart gave one enormous beat as he saw Eve walking very slowly up the aisle to him. Eve beamed; he smiled and winked at her. He mouthed, "I love you."

Even though Eve had her veil down, Martin could still see her mouthed back, "I love you."

She was all in violet, a bouquet of white flowers with one red rose. Eve had a short decorated veil. Next to her was her daughter Grace also in violet. His granddaughter Evelyn and her best friend Stacy walked behind as bridesmaids. Eve arrived next to him; he had stepped next to her. His son James was his best man. Bride and bridegroom faced each other as if they were in a dream; nothing and no one were in the church but them. Then the vicar cleared his throat, and the spell was broken; they faced him as he recited the marriage vows. One by one, he spoke, then Martin replied, then Eve replied. James gave his dad the ring. Eve offered her hand to Martin. Martin took her hand very shakily. He pushed the ring onto Eve's finger.

Somewhere someone said, "You are now man and wife. You may kiss the bride."

As this was stated, Martin and Eve hesitated for some time. Martin admired his bride Eve, not wishing this moment could end. Martin lifted the veil. "I love you, Eve." Then he kissed Eve; neither of them heard a single thing. It was as if the world stopped just for a moment.

Then all the noises bombarded them. They walked hand in hand along the aisle back to the door to the sunshine. They had their photograph taken. They awoke from this wonderful dream. Grace had James and Evelyn in her arms.

The congregation shouted out, "Throw the bouquet!"

Eve turned her back on everyone, gave one great big swing, and threw the bouquet in the air. Outstretched hands grappled for the flowers. One pair of hand caught the bouquet of flowers. Annabelle, the seamstress, caught them, held them close to her chest, and smelt the red rose.

The revellers moved into the main building for the reception.

Eve and her husband Martin sat hand in hand at the top of the main table. Evelyn and her friend Stacy earlier decorated the restaurant and foyer in violet and white streamers and bows; everyone celebrated the happy couple, speeches were made, wine flowed, then at a designated time, the happy couple arose from sitting to walk to their awaiting car. Giles and his mate affixed streamers from the window to the tip of the bonnet of the car. Willy had tied a small string of old boots to the bumper.

Martin got into the driver's seat, Eve next to him; they drove off to confetti and cheers of the party.

Eve and Martin had their honeymoon in Bay of Islands, a relaxing time after the wedding. On their return, they found that James had asked Grace to marry him. The wedding was set for later in the summer of the following year. For Eve and Martin, life settled into the usual. A number of villagers had grumbles of this and that; most were sorted out quite easily. One seemed more difficult and required Eve's and Martin's usual expertise. A Mr Nelson Brown was in the habit of turning his radio on very loudly in the evening. He was asked many times to turn his radio down but refused in rude terms, which offended Janis Grant. Once again, Eve and Martin took great pains to deal with the problem. Some weeks later, Janis had noticed that Nelson's radio hadn't been on at all. Getting quite worried about this, she asked the office manager to investigate.

They found Nelson next to his radio with his right hand on the on-off button. He had been electrocuted.

Once again, Eve and Martin had sorted out a difficult problem with their usual efficiency.

One morning, whilst Eve was having a shower, soaping her shoulders and allowing the soap bubbles to dribble down between her breasts, she felt it. Was it a bump? Was she mistaken? Eve stepped out of the shower and dried herself down. Martin had left to go down for a short walk before breakfast in the main building and was due to meet Eve after her shower.

Eve knew she was on her own in the apartment, so she stood facing the mirror in the bathroom. Investigating her left breast, Eve could feel a definite bump on the side of the nipple. Eve then felt around the right breast, and just under the nipple was another bump. Eve dressed and went downstairs to join Martin to have breakfast together. At the table, Eve made no mention of her problem. Eve had decided to see a doctor before talking to Martin about it. The doctor said Eve needed to see a specialist. The specialist examined her breasts and had an X-ray done, only to find all wasn't good. He informed her that she would only have a short time to go if she did not have extensive treatment.

After each treatment, she became far more sick; eventually, the specialist informed her that there was nothing more that could be done. The cancer had spread to her most of her body.

Eve and Martin took many walks along the cliffs in the park that was at the end of the main road.

One morning they stopped at the edge of the cliff. Eve turned to Martin. "Martin, I love you so much. I know I do not have very long to go."

Martin didn't answer her straight away but looked over the harbour to the other side, looking at the sea as it rolled to and fro; the seabirds swooping through the air.

"I will not live without you, my love."

They stood there looking at the waves crashing on the jagged rocks below; the spray wafting in the air. They were alone and in each other's arms as they stepped off the cliff. They plummeted to the rocks below. Neither of them felt the impact of the cruel rocks, just a sudden release of the body. They soared together into the far bend, lovers united in life and death.

Eternally yours.

CHAPTER 12

The following afternoon Lynda and Rascal, her two-year-old Jack Russell, were playing in the park with Lynda's new boyfriend John. He threw Rascal's ball this way then that, throwing the red ball high in the sky for Rascal to run barking as he went. "Catch, boy!"

John threw the ball to Lynda. She caught it then dropped it; the dog jumped greedily for the ball, racing away with it in his mouth. The couple ran after the dog, running this way then that; eventually, John caught the dog and the prized the ball out of his mouth. The dog barked, jumping up and down, spinning, dashing, trying to get the ball off John. He threw it in the air. "Go get it, Rascal!"

The ball got caught in the pine tree overhanging the cliff. The dog jumped up and down at the base of the tree, then with a bump, the tree released the captured ball, and it bounced over the top of the cliff.

The ball and the dog skidded down the cliff.

"John!" Lynda shouted. "Rascal has gone straight over the top of the cliff."

"I'll get him. He sounds okay. He is barking like crazy, Lynda."

"Rascal's probably found a dead seal on the rocks below, John."

"He did last weeks, Lynda, and he rolled in it too."

"John, I do wish he wouldn't do that. It's so hard to get that horrid smell off him."

"I'll go down the cliffs. I'll not be long, Lynda."

The dog was barking at something as the young man slipped and partway hung on to some tree roots, then at the bottom, he could see Rascal.

There on the rocks, he found them still hand in hand, gazing into each other's dead smiling eyes.

These two human beings truly loved each other. Even though they committed murder, love triumphs even in a desert of hate and murder.

You must make your own mind up.